MY BLEEDING HEART

MICHAEL KINGSWOOD

Copyright © 2019 by Michael Kingswood

Cover Art Copyright © NinaMalyna licensed through depositphotos.com

ISBN 13: 978-1-950683-11-6

ISBN 10: 1-950683-11-7

This story is a work of fiction. Names, characters, places, and incidents are either products of the author's imagination or used fictitiously. Any resemblance to actual events, locales, or persons, living or dead, is entirely coincidental.

All rights reserved.

No part of this book may be reproduced in any form or by any electronic or mechanical means, including information storage and retrieval systems, without written permission from the author, except for the use of brief quotations in a book review.

Parties interested in licensing rights to this property, should contact publisher@ssnstorytelling.com.

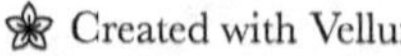 Created with Vellum

Contents

About This Book

Her name was Tabitha, and she tore my heart out and left me with a great, bleeding hole in my chest, while she walked away with an ear-to-ear smile.

Literally.

Finding out why would change my life forever.

My Bleeding Heart is a 4,700 word science fiction mystery.

Enjoy the book! After you're done, please come to Michael's website and sign up for his mailing list at michaelkingswood.com/newsletter-signup/. Guaranteed to be spam free, he uses it to announce new releases and special promotions for his fans.

My Bleeding Heart

Her name was Tabitha, and she tore my heart out and left me with a great, bleeding hole in my chest, while she walked away with an ear-to-ear smile.

Literally.

I was entranced by her from the moment we met. She was everything I'd ever wanted in a woman, physically. Small, curvy, but lean. Perky in every way - a perfect spinner. Plus she was a redhead, with the most sultry green eyes I'd ever seen. She dressed sexy all the time. And, wonder of wonders, she had a brain to boot.

And *she* approached *me*!

It seemed too good to be true. And, of course, it was. But I didn't find that out for almost a month. Until then, it was a torrid whirlwind of unbelievably awesome dates, incredible conversations, and mind-blowing sex that left me wondering how in the hell I had gotten so lucky.

All my friends were as mystified as I was. And not just because, as my friends, it was their job to give me shit. No, they were legitimately amazed at my good fortune, and, beneath all the required teasing, sincerely happy for me.

Then the phone call came.

"Tom, I need your help," she said, her voice quavering and husky, and not in a good way. She was upset, downright frightened, by something.

"What's wrong, babe?"

"I can't tell you over the phone. Can you meet me at the corner of Forest Glen and Maple in an hour?"

I looked at the time. It was four o'clock, and that place was halfway across town. I did some quick math in my head. If I left immediately, I could just make it. "Yeah, of course. What do you need?"

"Just you." I could hear legitimate need in her voice, desperation almost.

"Ok, I'm leaving now."

"Thanks, Tom." She paused for a heartbeat. "I love you."

That sent a rush of heat through my body, followed by a tingling that spread from my head to my toes. She had never said that before, and it should have scared me out of my wits to hear it. But coming from her right then, it felt good.

I couldn't bring myself to say it in return, though. It didn't matter, because she hung up before I could even try to. But that lack of follow-up, futile though it would have been, took the edge off the pleasure I felt from hearing it myself. The entire ride over to our rendezvous, I actually felt a little bit guilty about not saying it.

She was waiting at the corner when I got off the transit car half a block down, dressed in a more subdued manner than she ever had been: just jeans and a green t-shirt with a white shamrock and the words "O'Malley's Pub" on the back. She had her arms crossed beneath her breasts and was pacing with evident nerves, and her back was to me when I walked up.

When she turned around, our eyes met, and I saw that her shirt had a matching shamrock on the left breast. She managed a half-smile, and said, "Hi."

"Hey, what's going on? What do you need me to do?"

Her eyes left mine and moved to focus on something behind me. "You've already done it," she said.

I heard squealing tires a split second before something jabbed me in the side of the neck.

And then it all went black.

I DRIFTED SLOWLY in a world devoid of light or feeling, deeper than the deepest sleep, but somehow I was still aware that I was drifting. Until slowly, almost imperceptibly at first, input began registering with my senses. A beeping, almost too soft to hear. And was that a hint of a glow? A chill of cold, and then…

Crushing pain in my chest forced my eyes open. I would have screamed, but a contraption of some kind was holding my head steady and keeping my jaw from moving, while something round and hard was inserted down my throat. I could feel it running into my trachea.

Gag reflex tried to force the thing out, but no avail. It was stuck hard.

My limbs and torso were fixed, completely immobile; I could move only my eyes.

But all those discomforts were nothing compared with the sheer agony coming from my chest.

Agony such as I had never imagined, and cannot begin to describe in its fullness.

I looked around wildly, as best as I could without being able to move my head. In my torment, I could make out that I was on a bed of some kind, raised at a slight angle, and that the room I occupied was dingy, grey, but brightly lit. There were electronics of some kind off to the left, and a pair of tygon tubes running in a hanging apparatus from where the electronics sat to my chest. Both tubes were filled with red fluid.

"Oh shit, he's awake! How is he awake?"

I couldn't see the speaker, but there was panic in the man's voice. Footsteps approached me, then stopped.

"Forget it. There's no time."

I recognized that voice. A second later, Tabitha entered my field of view, dressed in surgical scrubs, with the requisite mask lowered below her chin so I could see it was her. She was smiling sweetly.

"You were supposed to be out until the police arrive." She shook her head and, pursing her lips, leaned down and kissed my forehead. "Sorry about that," she breathed.

Tabitha straightened, turned, and walked away. "Have a nice day," I heard from her. And then two sets of footsteps reached my ears, followed by the sound of a door closing.

I was alone, needing to scream, but completely unable to.

THE COPS DIDN'T SHOW up for almost an hour, but to me it was a century. Or perhaps a millennium. Or six. It's impossible to describe if you haven't gone through it.

And who has ever been awake, conscious and feeling, with their chest ripped open and their heart literally torn out?

It should not have been possible for me to be awake. They had put me on a bypass machine and intubated me to keep me alive while they took my heart. I supposed that made them feel like they were being more humane. Or something. But I should not have been awake, or even close to it.

But I was. And it was pure hell.

It took almost as long for the paramedics to arrive after the cops reached me. When they finally did, I was jumping out of my skin from the sheer torment of it all. I didn't even feel it when they stuck the needle in, I just welcomed the drowsiness that quickly washed over me.

As I drifted off to sleep again, I wished that I would never wake.

***

BUT WAKE I DID. Two weeks later.

When I opened my eyes, I was, to be honest, completely surprised. I truly had not expected to ever see the world again.

I was in the standard hospital room: subdued colors, fluorescent lights, medical instruments everywhere, uncomfortable chairs for visitors, and bad artwork on the walls.

More important, from my perspective, the pain in my chest was muted, down to a low, continuous throb. And I felt a pulse in my neck as I breathed normally, without a tube down my throat.

It was like heaven.

Except, of course, that it wasn't. My heart was still gone, stolen, and the crushing violation of that event weighed on my mind like a ton of bricks.

Since there was neither donor available nor time to grow a new one, the Doctors had replaced my real heart with a mechanical model. It was clunky and inefficient, and would never allow the range of activity that a flesh and blood unit could, but it was something, and it kept me alive.

For a long time, I wished it had not.

How to describe the enormity of what had been done to me? The physical effects are obvious; I left the hospital a week later with a full understanding of what they were and how to adapt to my new limitations.

But everywhere I went, I was jumpy. I flinched at shadows, and God help you if you walked up to me from behind and clapped me on my shoulder.

And women…

Don't get me started about women.

The worst part is the cops had no leads. Not one. Tabitha and I had always ever met out and came back to her place. But it turned out her place was a flat rented on a day-to-day basis, and had been cleaned to surgical bay standards. Not a trace of DNA or any physical evidence of any sort remained there. Nor were there any electronic leads to follow. I hadn't noticed it at the time, because the entire time I was there we had been engaged in…other pursuits, but there was no network connection, no wireless connection, of any kind in the flat, and no electrons left behind. Finally, the entity that had rented the place was, of course, fake and untraceable.

Even the room where I had been found, in the back of a long-abandoned warehouse, was pristine.

The equipment they used had been reported stolen from a local hospital two weeks earlier, but when the cops pulled the string on that, again there was not a hint as to who did it.

It was like Tabitha and her accomplice were ghosts; they had vanished without a trace. And I was left wondering how to put the pieces of my life back together again.

How could I go back to being what I was?

THE ANSWER, of course, was, "very badly."

It wasn't long before I lost my job. I could tell it killed my boss to let me go, but I couldn't blame him. I knew I was fucked up, and I was a drain on his company's resources, not a benefit. But it still sucked.

I ended up working at a grocery store, re-stocking shelves. It was easy, mind-numbing work, and that's what I needed right then: something to just turn off my brain so I could run on autopilot and not think. Because thinking always brought me back to that room, and that was the last place I needed to go back to.

But no matter what, it seemed that I could not leave. Every time I took my shirt off and beheld the scar, it all came back to me.

Booze didn't help. Drugs didn't help. I was scraping rock bottom, and I knew it. But I couldn't think of a way to move on.

Until I received the note.

I stumbled into my dingy, cramped flat in the basement of a building that was barely a step above a tenement and collapsed into my thread-bare excuse for a stuffed chair, head swimming from the fifth of cheap whiskey that I had made a serious dent in on my way home from work. I hardly noticed when the bottle slipped out of my hand and landed on the faux-wood floor with a dull thud, teetered, then fell over, spilling the remains of my attempt at healing. Any other day, I might have mustered the energy to pick it back up before the booze was all lost, but that night I just let myself drift off to sleep.

The first thing I noticed when I woke was the splitting headache and creeping nausea that always follows a bender with bad booze. The second was that my door was standing wide open.

I blinked, brain still fuzzy. Had I closed it when I came in? I couldn't remember.

Not that it mattered. I didn't have anything worth stealing, and if someone had wanted to kill me...

I chuckled ruefully at how I welcomed that thought and pushed myself up onto my feet. There I swayed for a minute, whatever remained of last night's dinner threatening to come up right then and there from the sudden change in my body's equilibrium.

That's when I noticed it. A memo-sized white envelope lying on the floor just inside the door. There was no return address or postage on it, no identifying features at all except for my name, printed in large, plain letters.

Confusion mixed with curiosity as I stepped over, squatted down, and picked the envelope up. It was light and thin, the paper coarse. Frowning, I ripped the tab open and withdrew the contents.

The first was a plain white sheet of paper. Written on it in the same plain font as had been on the envelope were the words, "You are not the only one."

A chill went down my spine as I dropped the page and looked at the printed photo that lay beneath.

It was her, sitting at a streetside cafe with some poor schlub I had never seen before: a guy in his thirties with light brown hair and a round, cherub-like face. From her posture and his expression, I was pretty sure she was putting the moves on him, and he was eating it up, just like I had.

Beneath that photo was a second, showing her ascending the stairs to the front door of a brownstone-style apartment building, sans cherub-man. The building very kindly had a label over its door: 252 San Luzelle Avenue.

And that was it. I double-checked the envelope and found nothing else. Not even a hint of who had sent it and why.

I sat back on my butt and picked up the photo of her at the cafe again. The chill turned into a growing heat within me that burned away the last of my buzz from last night, and at least some of my hangover.

Finally, I had a way forward.

TURNS out there are five hundred fifteen San Luzelle Avenues in the world. I wouldn't have thought that before I started looking. But it wasn't too terribly hard to narrow down to the one I was looking for with the ubiquitous mapping applications that infest the network. It just took time, and what else did I have to do? Bag groceries?

I didn't bother. Instead I just focused on her, and a couple days later, I knew where she was: a thousand kilometers away, near the coast.

I had a fair amount of money in the bank before this all started, but I hadn't bothered to check my balance in a while. I had 600 credits left. Just enough to buy a suborbital hop.

And a gun.

IT'S HARDER to stake out a building than I would have thought.

I had no car, only the clothes on my back and the supplies in my backpack. So just standing around on the sidewalk would have been suspicious. So would walking back and forth on the same block over and over. Someone would have eventually noticed and called the cops. And what was I going to tell them, that I had received an anonymous tip about the location of a woman they hadn't been able to find?

They'd think I was nuts. Or at the very least they would—rightly—think I meant her harm and throw me in the clink instead of her.

So I had to be circumspect, and risk missing her. But I didn't see much choice in the matter. I went down her block every twenty minutes to half hour, changing sides of the sidewalk and donning and doffing a different shirt, or a sweater, each time. I kept my shades on and did my best to not obviously ogle her building. But I had no training or experience in that sort of thing, and I got the distinct impression I was receiving suspicious looks after a few hours of that routine.

If had to keep it up much longer, I would have had to figure a different method. But I got lucky.

The sun was beginning to set behind the buildings opposite hers, and the shadows had lengthened so that I didn't feel quite so conspicuous. I was maybe a hundred paces away from her door on the opposite side of the street when it opened.

And she walked out.

She was just as small and perky as I remembered, but as it was getting on toward autumn she wasn't dressed as revealingly as she had been when

I knew her. She wore jeans instead of shorts or a skirt, and a lavender sweater that set off her hair nicely. But she was just as sexy, and had that same self-confident walk as she had when I first met her.

My hands clenched into fists, and I had to restrain myself from sprinting over there and beating her senseless right there on the street.

I distinctly felt the weight of the gun, in its holster inside the waistband of my pants, calling out to be used.

Patience, I told myself. Get someplace private, and then...

I had not done much smiling over the last several months. The skin of my face felt like it was cracking, so unused to the expression was it.

A guy walking toward me on the sidewalk glanced at my face and then abruptly veered to his right to avoid me, wearing a look of alarm.

Soon, now.

Soon.

I FOLLOWED HER ON FOOT, being careful not to get too close as she wended her way through the sidewalk traffic. Aside from being spotted, my biggest concern was that she would get in a car or hop a transport, but she never did.

For forty-five minutes we walked, leaving the well-manicured residential area where she lived and heading into a more commercial region. Boutiques and cafes yielded to industrial supply stores, business headquarters, and warehouses, and it was into one of the later that she, finally, turned.

The place was rather small for a warehouse, and lacked any signs to indicate who owned it or what businesses used it. That didn't surprise me; if she kept to the process she used for me, this place would probably be completely deserted.

She entered through a side-door about two-thirds of the way down the building on its left side. I hung back, around the corner where I could watch without being seen, until she was inside, then I hurried to catch up.

The door was grey, matching the peeling paint on the building's siding, and had a small window in its upper half. I peeked in and saw a narrow hallway leading straight away from the door. No lights on.

I tried the knob, and it turned.

Sloppy of her to not lock up behind herself. My face cracked again as I stepped inside.

Compared with the streets outside, the building was almost oppressively silent. It smelled of dust, and there was a chill in the air above and beyond the coolness of the encroaching autumn night outside.

I let the door shut slowly behind me, easing it to minimize any noise, and listened.

A few seconds later, I thought I heard a thud and soft footsteps from ahead. Nodding to myself, I reached beneath my shirt, drew my gun, and started forward.

The hallway veered to the right, and I passed two closed doors. I stopped to listen at each, but, hearing nothing, I continued on. Finally the hallway ended, and I faced a choice: a glass door that opened into a large room filled with storage shelves, the warehouse proper, or a set of stairs heading up to the left.

There was too much visibility for the sort of thing she had planned on the warehouse floor. I went up.

As I neared the top of the stairs, I heard another thump, followed by a muttered curse.

I recognized the voice.

My smile widened.

I found her in a moderate-sized room near the rear of the building. Windowless, it had probably been a storeroom of some kind, but now its only furnishings were a raised bed at the far side and several large boxes over to the right. I had no doubt what was in those boxes.

Tabitha was fiddling with something near the head of the bed, I could not see what. And, frankly, I didn't care. Her back was to me, and that was enough.

I raised the gun and sighted in on the center of her back. I almost squeezed the trigger.

But I needed some answers first.

"This is where you're going to do it."

She stiffened as I spoke, and for a second I thought she was going to bolt. Instead, she turned around, slowly. As our eyes met, surprise flooded her pretty features.

"Tom," she said, and I was frankly amazed she remembered my name. "What are you doing here?"

I took a step closer, keeping the sights centered on her chest. "What's it look like?"

I had to hand it to her, if having a gun trained on her gave her pause, she did not show it. "Oh, you're not still sore over that are you?"

In point of fact, I was. Even though I had long since healed, I did still get the occasional twinge from my breastbone. And, of course, that mechanical pump in my chest never did feel completely…right. But that wasn't what she meant, and we both knew it.

Right then, I really wished my gun wasn't

striker fired, so it would have a hammer I could cock. Instead, I just scowled at her. "Why'd you do it?"

She kept her eyes locked on mine and stepped forward languidly, trailing the fingertips of her left hand on the top of the mattress. I remembered how she used to run those fingers up and down on my back. She had been good at that.

"Oh come on, Tom. It was nothing personal. Just business. You met the parameters, is all." Her lips curled upward every so slightly into a smokey little smile. "For what it's worth, you were my favorite supplier." Her tone had changed to match that smile, and despite the utter hatred for her that I held in what passed for my heart, I felt my pants begin to tighten.

My God, she was sexy when she wanted to be.

Still, it wasn't all that hard to remain focused. "Business? Whose business?"

She took another step forward. "We don't exchange names. I'm sure you can understand why." Those eyes burrowed into mine, and I felt sweat begin to trickle down my brow in spite of the room's chill.

I swallowed. "Don't come any closer."

That smile widened. "Why? We both know you're not going to shoot me." Her lips parted, and her tongue moved slowly, sensuously over them. "Why don't you put the gun down, and we'll break the bed in," she patted her hand down on the mattress. "Once more, for old time's sake?" She raised one eyebrow.

I almost did it. I almost gave in.

But then I noticed that her hand was lying right next to a folded up blanket, and that blanket had a little lump in it.

My gun had lowered as my determination

waned. I got ahold of myself and raised it back up, and her hand darted beneath the blanket.

I fired.

She did not cry out as the bullet impacted her chest. She just looked at me, features locked into an expression of utter surprise.

I shot again.

She fell in a heap. The gun that had been hidden under the blanket landed next to her, clattering on the linoleum floor.

I just stood there, surrounded by a little cloud of gun smoke, and looked at her dead body.

It was probably the most satisfying thing I have ever done.

I WAS STILL STANDING THERE when they arrived.

Three men in black tactical gear, rifles at the ready and balaclavas covering their faces, stormed into the room, diverting around me and sweeping the area with the sights of their weapons before one of them said, "Clear," in a loud, confident voice.

They never pointed their weapons at me, but I thought it prudent to drop my gun anyway. Then I placed my hands behind my head and waited to be handcuffed.

Instead, a man's voice from behind me said, "Not bad, Tom. Thought we were going to have to load you on another gurney for a second there, but you came through."

Steady footsteps, and then a man in a black suit, black dress shoes, a white shirt and a black tie stepped into my field of view from behind. Of course, he worse black sunglasses.

I looked askance at him, still keeping my hands behind my head. "What are you supposed to be? Feds?"

The man shrugged. "Something like that." He looked around the room, his gaze lingering on Tabitha's body for a second. He sniffed. "I would have preferred to take her alive, but considering..." He shrugged again, then looked back at me. "I suppose I can't blame you. We're taking her partner now. I expect we'll get what we need from him."

"You sent the note."

The left side of the man's lips turned upward into a half-almost-smile.

"Why?"

He considered me for a long moment, then seemed to come to a decision of sorts as he nodded ever so slightly. "You're not the only one who's been...violated. There's been a rash of these sorts of attacks all over the world."

"Why?" I felt like I was repeating myself.

He shrugged. "No idea, to be honest. Between the grow-vats and mechanical substitutes, there's no shortage of replacement organs available to those who need them." He pursed his lips. "No, there's something else going on here. "We," he gestured toward his men, who had remained silent the entire time, "are part of a special Task Force, assigned to get to the bottom of it."

I snorted. "Then why am I doing your job for you?"

I could feel his disdainful stare through the lenses of his shades. His lips compressed, and for a second I thought he was going to shout at me. Instead, he spoke in a level tone. "We took at look at your background, and thought you might be of some use to us. So we gave you a try out." The half-grin returned. "Which you passed."

I blinked, surprised.

"So how about it? Want a job?"

"Doing what, exactly?"

His eyebrows rose. "Not stocking groceries, I can promise you that."

I had to admit, that stung.

"I'm giving you a chance to help make sure what happened to you doesn't happened to anyone else ever again."

"I thought I just did."

It was his turn to snort. "This was one crew, in one corner of the world. We are certain there are others. Many others." He paused, then added. "How about this? You do good by us, we'll do good by you. Replace that mechanical ticker with a real one. What do you say?"

To be frank, I would have said yes even without that added extra benefit. I nodded.

"Good."

"You gonna tell me your name?"

I half expected him to say "Agent Smith." Instead, he said, "Boris Donnegal. Special Agent in Charge." He extended his hand, and we shook. "Welcome to Task Force Phoenix, Mr. Douglass."

WE LEFT TOGETHER, and the next day I arrived in a compound, somewhere, that they used for training.

Donnegal tells me it'll be three months of training in their protocols and procedures before I'll be allowed out into the field again. The training has been tough, and I find I can't get enough of it. For the first time in a long while, I have something to focus on besides my own brutalization. He offered a mission, but I found so much more. A rebirth, a new life. And a chance to meet revenge on the one pulling the strings.

I can't wait.

Message From The Author

Thank you for reading my book. I hope you enjoyed reading it as much as I enjoyed writing it.

Every review helps an author out, so whether you loved this book, hated it, or something in between, please take a minute to tell other readers what you thought. All of the online retailers make it very easy to do, and I would really appreciate it.

Feel free to come say hi at my website or on Facebook. I always enjoy hearing from readers, especially since you all are, collectively, my boss.

I also have a weekly podcast, Story Time With Michael Kingswood, where I read stories and talk through some of the latest goings on in my world. I'd love to see you there.

Thanks again. My best to you and yours.

Warm Regards,
Michael Kingswood

Mailing List

If you enjoyed this book and would like word on new releases and special deals from Michael Kingswood, sign up for his newsletter on his website. Guaranteed to be spam-free, you can opt out at any time. And you can rest assured he will not share your information with anyone, for any reason.

https://michaelkingswood.com/newsletter-signup/

Supporting Patronage

Michael would like to invite you to become a supporting member of his website. Similar in concept to Patreon, a few dollars a month will give you access to exclusive content, and help him to focus more of his time to writing fun and exciting stories for your enjoyment.

Sign up at his website:

https://www.michaelkingswood.com/
membership/supporting-patronage/

About The Author

Michael Kingswood is 20-year veteran of the US Navy submarine force and a lifelong fan of science fiction and fantasy literature. His work has appeared in numerous collections and anthologies, to include the Fiction River Anthology series from WMG publishing. He holds a bachelors degree in Mechanical Engineering as well as a Master of Engineering Management and a Master of Business Administration. He has four children and currently resides in San Diego.

Find Michael Kingswood online at:

www.michaelkingswood.com

www.facebook.com/michael.kingswood

steemit.com/@michaelkingswood

Glimmer Vale Chronicles

Glimmer Vale

Out-Dweller

Tollard's Peak

Robbed Blind

Wedding Gifts: A Glimmer Vale Chronicles Story

The Falconer's Stairs

Glimmer Vale Omnibus Edition #1

The Pericles Conspiracy

Passing In The Night

The Pericles Conspiracy

Dawn Of Enlightenment

Masters Of The Sun

Novellas

What Lurks Between

The Necromancer's Lair

The Champion

Veritas Morte

Story Collections

Tales Of Adventure #1

Tales Of Adventure #2

Short Story 10-Pack

A Jar Of Mixed Treats

Short Fiction

Michael has also published a number of shorter works,
links to which can be found on his website.

www.ingramcontent.com/pod-product-compliance
Lightning Source LLC
Chambersburg PA
CBHW032054180726
48284CB00004B/1330